The Adventures of Petey the Pelican

Doug Lampman

authorHOUSE®

AuthorHouse™
1663 Liberty Drive
Bloomington, IN 47403
www.authorhouse.com
Phone: 1 (800) 839-8640

Published by AuthorHouse 01/21/2019

ISBN: 978-1-5462-5675-5 (sc)
ISBN: 978-1-5462-5674-8 (e)

Library of Congress Control Number: 2018910027

Dedication

This story is dedicated to my son Brett, my daughters Maeve and Tatum, my Mom, my friend Eric and anyone else who wonders. Like Goggles said, "With wonder comes experiences both good and bad, but also with wonder comes a rich and fulfilling life."

Authors' note

I have always enjoyed looking at Pelicans. They seem so deep in thought and relaxed. When I lived in Florida I would sit with them while I fished off local piers. My son Brett was two years old at the time and loved to hear stories while we traveled about in my truck. Petey the Pelican was born during these storytelling times. Petey would preach of safety, respect and other things a two year old needs to know. Many years later, while taking a writing class with Brett, he requested I write a story about Petey. Since we now live in Surprise, NY, it seemed fitting to bring Petey to us, at our lake, so we could enjoy a pelican again. Maybe someday Petey will come. My hope is you will enjoy this story and be a better friend to someone because of it.

Special thanks

To my son Brett for listening to me, suggesting names of and developing characters for this story.

My two daughters, Maeve and Tatum for encouraging me to publish.

My wife Stephanie for her support.

To my editors Jean Heiberg and Lorraine Ferrara.

To my illustrators Ned and Wendy for bringing the characters to life.

To all my family and friends that make life so fulfilling.

1

Petey's Big Decision

The day started like all the rest, the soft glow of sunlight growing into morning. As the mist lifted, the sounds of boats in the harbor and the gentle lapping of water on his pier, caused Petey to awake. As Petey did every morning, he opened his sleepy eyes and stretched his wings. His friend Horace was already aloft, he could see him over the blue water diving for his breakfast. Petey would usually be the first to catch a morning air current and join Horace at the vast breakfast buffet called Tampa Bay but this morning he was content to just think. And think he did. What should he do?

Petey was a pelican; if you asked anyone who knew him they would say he was a good pelican, with one problem- he thought too much. He did not let his thinking get him down, but he was always wondering. He wondered about how the bay was filled with water, where all the fish came from, what was passed all those stars in the sky, what was life like outside of his bay and what was the meaning of his life. Most of his friends did not wonder. Most of his friends woke up, searched for food, gossiped with one another, and then went to sleep. One friend did not.

Petey met Goggles quite by accident. On some days Petey would sit at the end of the great pier on Bradenton Beach and visit with an old man who fished there often. The old man would sit on a bucket and fish the early morning and then go home. Most days he would put his catch in his bucket to bring it home. But on some days he would toss one to Petey, which was always appreciated. Petey enjoyed sitting next to the old man even if he did not give him fish. Petey would wonder about the man, what did he do off the pier, did he have a family and what were these songs he was always singing? On the day Petey met Goggles a girl came up to the man crying. She was sobbing as she spoke to the man. The man had concern on his face and walked briskly to his car with the girl. As they left the parking lot, Petey decided to follow them. Over the causeway bridges, the car drove as Petey watched from aloft. The car drove for quite a while, Petey was so focused on the car that he did not realize he could no longer see the bay. Finally the car pulled into a driveway, so Petey circled the house. Finding no place to land, he splashed down in a small pond behind the house. Petey watched from the pond as the little girl's mother put a band-aid on her finger and kissed her hand. The old man's concern was no longer on his face, as he sipped his lemonade on the front porch.

Petey was startled as a huge splash landed just inches behind him. When the shards of water cleared, a large Canadian goose was sitting there. And he did not look happy. "How dare you land in my pond!" shouted the goose, "You have no business here."

"I'm sorry," said Petey, "I had no where else to land, besides there is nothing wrong with sharing."

Goggles looked at Petey and hissed, "I don't share with Salties, and you're a Salty." Petey wondered what was meant by a Salty.

"My name is Petey, not Salty, what is yours?"

"I do not share Or talk to Salties, so fly back to your home."

"Fine," said Petey, "but not before you tell me what a Salty is."

"A Salty is a bird who never leaves the bay, born in the bay, stays in the bay, dies in the bay. How many times have you left the bay?" asked Goggles.

"This is my first," replied Petey.

"See, I told you- you are a Salty!"

"Fine, I'm a Salty, what are you?" asked Petey.

"I'm a migratory, I see the world as I travel, no sitting in one place for me."

Petey immediately perked up, travel he thought. "Could you share with me where you have been?" asked Petey.

Goggles loved to talk about his adventures, even if it was with this annoying intruder. His tone and expression softened and he held out his wing, "Goggles is the name, I suppose I could share some of my adventures."

Well, when Goggles started, there was no stopping him. For the rest of the day Goggles shared exciting stories about all the places he had been. Stories of the great foreign land of Canada, the lovely coast of Carolina, the towering buildings in New York City and his favorite pond in a place called Surprise, NY. He returns to this pond every year. There are children who come to play, there are wildlife that visit and it is so peaceful. At night the stars shine down as the moon rises and sounds of night animals fill the air. Goggles admitted that it is not the fanciest place in the world, but he feels most at peace when he is there.

On that first afternoon, time flew for Petey. Finally, he said he must be going, "Horace will wonder where I have been, may I stop by again, I want to hear more?"

"You know where my pond is," said Goggles, "come back any time."

So Petey did. For the next few months Petey left his Bay and flew to Goggle's pond almost every day. He spent his days listening to Goggles and his nights sharing the stories with Horace. Time flew and the sun grew hotter.

One day Goggles told Petey he had to go. Petey did not understand, "Where are you going?" asked Petey.

"It is time for me to fly back to the North to see my family and friends," said Goggles.

"But I don't want you to go," said Petey, "I will miss our talks."

"I will miss them too," said Goggles, "but traveling is what I do, so

I must go-one flock already flew up the coast, I do not want to miss the next one."

Petey was silent, then he spoke "Will you be back?" he asked.

"Sure," said Goggles, "when the sun cools down, I will return as I do every year. Petey, I have to ask you something."

"What is it?"

"Would you like to come with me for this adventure?" Petey gasped with shock and excitement, but then quickly lowered his gaze wearing an expression of doubt.

When he spoke, he did so hesitantly "How, I couldn't, I mean, is that possible?"

"Of course" said Goggles, "you will be with me; we can catch the prevailing winds and be in Surprise with my family in three weeks, besides you fly better than I do." Petey did not know what to say, he managed to stammer, "I do not know, let me think about it, can I let you know later?"

"It better be soon." said Goggles, "I am leaving on the next flock out of here."

"I'll see you tomorrow, said Petey, "do not leave until I return."

"You got it," said Goggles, "see you tomorrow."

Petey flew off.

Petey spent the night thinking. He knew he wanted to go, but could he make it? He had never been out of the bay before he met Goggles. This was too much, but on the other hand, if he did not go, he would always wonder. Through most of the night, Petey sat on his pier and thought, finally he fell asleep.

As the sun rose, Petey opened his eyes and stretched his wings. Horace was already fishing out in front of him, floating high in the sky looking for his morning breakfast. Normally Petey would join him, but this morning he needed to think. What should he do? Is he really a Salty? Time and a quiet night had not been enough to give him a decision.

Just then Horace landed in the water next to Petey.

"Hey Petey, the Mullet are all schooled up by the Anna Maria Pier. It is crazy over there. All you see is fish flipping out of the water and the gang diving into the water. I love a feeding frenzy at low tide. Bungles still can't work the low tide, he slammed head first into two inches of water and skinned the feathers off his head."

"Good morning, Horace," said Petey, even the weighty decision on his mind could not keep him from smiling at the thought of Bungles slamming the bottom. Smiling he added, "good old Bungles, if he needed a license to fly they would take it away."

"Do you want to fly over to the Sunshine Skyway today?" asked Horace, "There is the annual fishing derby- nothing like stealing some bait and catch."

Petey did not answer. Horace paddled closer, "You look like you did not sleep a wink," said Horace, "what are you thinking about now Petey?"

Petey was still silent. Finally he raised his head and asked Horace "Do you think I could fly away from the bay?"

"Sure you could," said Horace, "you do it all the time to see Goggles."

"No, I mean really fly away, with the migratories."

Horace's waddle flapped as he cocked his head to the side, "what do you mean Petey?" he said.

"I mean fly up the coast with Goggles and his flock, see all the places that Goggles told me about."

Now it was Horace's turn to be silent.

Petey continued, "We would fly straight up the coast, probably where all those boats go, and then fly to a pond that Goggles goes to. He said we could be there in a few weeks, but I do not know. Goggles said he has never seen a pelican in New York, so I may be the first. I would also have to eat frogs-whatever they are."

Horace's face broke into a wide grin, "Well," he said, "this deserves a going away party. I am going to get the gang together and we are spending the day at the Skyway."

"Wait," said Petey, "I did not say I was going yet."

Horace jumped out of the water and landed on the pier next to Petey. "Petey, listen," Horace said. "Ever since I met you, you have been spending time thinking about what is out there; you are a great friend but a very curious pelican. If you do not take this opportunity to answer some of those questions, you will regret it all your life. Go, you must, then come back and tell me all about it."

Petey stretched his wings and with a big hop jumped into the morning air while Horace watched. He climbed up and away from the docks, and then began to circle back. Gliding in, he landed next to Horace with a splash.

"You're right Horace. I am going to go. I must let Goggles know, I will be back later, get the gang together, we are going to harass some fishermen at the Skyway."

Petey did not stay long, Goggles was very excited to hear the news, Goggles suggested Petey get some rest tonight and eat as much as he could. The flock leaves in the morning from Longboat Key.

"Don't party too much," said Goggles with a smile.

Petey spent the day with the gang, stealing bait, eating the catch and dive bombing into all the fishing schools- much to the fishermen's frustration. Bungles got himself tangled into the fishing line of three fishermen and managed to knock into the water a fishing rod. If the owner's reaction was any indication, the rod and reel were expensive. As the day wore down, Petey said his goodbyes and flew back to his pier. On his flight, he thought to himself, 'I doubt I will meet friends like these on my adventure.'

2
Petey Prepares for Departure

Petey did as Goggles told him, and slept all night. The sun's light was just showing over the horizon as he woke up on his pier. He was surprised to see a shape on the horizon getting closer and closer. Due to the darkness, the form was right on him before he recognized his friend, Horace.

"Horace," said Petey, "what are you doing up so early?"

"I could not let my friend leave without a send off from his buddy, besides I am just getting back from the Skyway party; those boys know how to party all night," said Horace.

Petey smiled to himself. "Well old friend, what time are you heading out?" asked Horace.

"Shortly," replied Petey, "I told Goggles I would be up to Longboat Key by sunrise."

"How are you going to find this pond in New York? It seems so far," asked Horace.

"That is a great question," Petey replied, "one I asked Goggles. He said that every year he flies behind the same three flock leaders. They always know the time to fly, where to fly, when to push the flock or when to rest. The flock leaders are the bravest, smartest and most trusted by the flock. It takes them many years to earn the flock's trust and they never get lost or make bad decisions."

"Seems like a lot of pressure to me," said Horace.

"Goggles said you can never talk to them or you will be sent out of the V. It is real hard to keep up with them out of the V, usually you are never allowed back in."

"Just for talking to them Petey? that seems silly."

"Hey Horace, we are Pelicans, not Geese, so who are we to judge. Anyway, one of the flock leaders is Goggles' uncle, I am sure we will be well taken care of."

Horace yawned.

"Petey," said Horace, "I am tired so I will bid thee farewell. I cannot wait to hear all your stories when you return. I will be thinking of you and I wish you good luck. I hope you get the answers to some of the questions you have been wondering about."

"Thanks," said Petey, "I will miss you and the boys too. Tell Bungles we will practice his low tide work when I return."

"Why help him?" asked Horace, "It is so funny watching him come out of the water with seaweed, mud and no feathers on his head."

The two friends had a laugh together, slapped wings, and Horace flew off. Petey could hear him yell as he flew away, "Use lots of salt on them frogs."

After Horace disappeared, Petey looked around his pier, shook his head, and jumped into the air. Longboat Key was a ten-minute flight that Petey was never aware of because all he could think about was what a great group of friends he had here in the bay.

3
Petey Meets His Traveling Party

When Petey flew over the city of Sarasota and saw the flock gathered on the beach, his first impression was how loud the flock was on such a quiet morning. He could hear them from two miles away, just honking and squawking. His second thought was, "How the heck was he going to find Goggles in all these geese?" Petey made one circle and then landed in the middle of the flock next to the water's edge.

In the next three seconds, everything changed. To Petey's misfortune, that loud honking and squawking turned to total silence and all eyes turned toward Petey. This helped answer his second question; it would not be hard to find Goggles because Goggles would find him. The whole flock was focused on the awkward-looking Pelican standing in the sand at the water's edge. It may have only been ten seconds, but to Petey it felt like an eternity. As his heart rate quickened, he heard the far off sounds of a familiar voice.

"Petey, over here, over here!" Goggles shouted as others moved out of his way.

"Boy am I glad to see you Goggles, I think I crashed your going away party."

"Aw, don't worry about these cackling balls of feathers, they are just following instincts. Look, we are leaving in a couple of minutes, are you feeling strong?"

"Absolutely," said Petey, "are you sure I am allowed to go?"

"Just stay in the V, mind your own business and everything will be fine. Oh, do NOT talk to the flock leaders. Got it?"

"Got it," said Petey.

After much more honking, some squawking and a little bickering, one by one the geese began to take to the air. They would fly out over the bay and circle waiting for the rest of their flock. Petey jumped aloft and tried to match flaps and glides with his new partners. With some practice, he was able to move at a similar speed. With no obvious warning, the geese aloft began to assemble. At first one would not believe it was happening, but after a while it became obvious- the flock was born. The three flock leaders took their place in the front and an obvious V formed behind them. It looked like every other V of geese you have ever seen flying north for the summer, but with one tiny difference- there was a pelican in the formation.

The first few hours were amazing. Petey felt like a pelican reborn. Over each city, around every island, and over all the bridges, Petey experienced a new sight. He never thought so much was just outside his bay. He wondered all morning about the creatures he flew over, about what was ahead and about what he left behind. His wondering helped fuel his thumping wing beats; each wing beat represented a new and exciting experience. Petey could feel the V moving as one; in unison his traveling companions matched their motions and moved in a steady pace. Occasionally one would drift out of formation and fall back immediately. Petey remembered what Goggles said, "do not leave the formation, you will work very hard to get back in." Petey was not worried about that, he felt strong and happy. Any previous reservations had been replaced by sheer exhilaration.

As the day wore on, so did the flock, until finally Goggles pulled up next to Petey and yelled, "Won't be long now, the leaders are looking for a place to land."

Petey, yanked out of his daydream, managed to nod.

Soon the V began a downward descent toward a pond that seemed quiet enough. As Petey came down he saw off in the distance the remarkable sight of many lights shining through the night air and crowds of people moving around. Petey landed like all the rest on the remote and quiet pond.

When Goggles splashed next to Petey, Petey asked, "What were those brilliant lights as we were landing?"

"Oh, they are fireworks and lasers. They do that every night at this place. My friend once told me the people are celebrating a mouse."

"That's funny… a mouse?" Petey thought out loud. Petey would never remember his first night with his traveling companions; he was asleep while some were still landing.

4
Petey Gets Lucky

P etey was dreaming that a fish was stuck in his waddle. Back and forth the fish swam. Then he was dreaming that an ant was walking down his beak. It walked down and up. His dream changed to a great wind blowing on his face. The wind was a pure Salty breeze that made his feathers- wait a second, this wind smelled like pond muck. Petey's dream disappeared, and his sleep haze lifted. What he saw helped explain the dream. The little duck swam under Petey and flapped his waddle; then he ran his wing feathers down his beak and finally he blew as hard as he could into his face. After Petey saw what was happening, he opened both eyes and opened his mouth as wide as he could and snapped at the duck. The duck, expecting full well that Petey was asleep, almost had a heart attack. Quacking and scrambling, he retreated away from Petey in a blur.

Petey laughed, "Good morning little fellow." The mallard duck peered out of the rushes.

"I'm not afraid of you, you fish-breath, long-beaked, flappy-throated bird, I'm sure not!"

"I doubt you are, but I did get you pretty good," said Petey.

"I knew you were going to do that; I just wanted to mess with you," said the duck swimming closer.

"My name is Petey," said the yawning pelican.

The duck swam up to Petey, in front of him was a young mallard duck, trim, fit and with two feathers sticking straight up on his head.

"My name is Lucky, at least that is what they call me around here. Hey, why are you here with the migratories; aren't you a Salty?" asked Lucky.

Any first impression respect left Petey's voice. "I am not a Salty," said Petey, "I live in Tampa Bay- do you know where that is?," asked Petey, "I did not think so," said Petey abruptly.

"I have never seen a pelican flying with geese, that's all, you look out of place."

Petey composed himself and replied, "I am no ordinary Pelican, I'm a pioneer."

"Well," said Lucky, "you do not look like a pioneer; you look rather out of place."

"Fine, that is your opinion. Shouldn't such a young duck as yourself have someone around that is watching over you?" asked Petey scanning the area.

Lucky looked at Petey, spit in the water in front of him and said, "I'm not so little, and you're not the boss of me- so drop dead Pelican!"

Lucky shot Petey a sour look and paddled away. As Lucky turned the corner of the cattails, Petey was startled to see his friend, Goggles.

Goggles exclaimed, "What a crummy place to spend the night. Last year we were much farther north than this. Something about the wind currents holding us back. I heard earlier that we are stuck here all day; the leaders do not want to fly until the wind changes- too hard for the young ones. This is ridiculous."

"Good morning to you to Goggles, did we paddle out of the wrong side of the bed?"

Goggles looked at Petey and was not amused.

"Have you ever been here before?" asked Petey.

"Yes, we stayed over at this pond on our way home last fall. Why?"

"Well," said Petey, "I just met a duck, a little duck with a big attitude. I was wondering if you knew who he was."

"I don't but I probably know someone who does," suggested Goggles.

"There used to be a gopher who lived on the north shore of the pond," continued Goggles, "I only know him because I was feeding along the banks and stepped in his hole. He was not happy to be disturbed, but he was a lonely gopher looking for someone to talk to."

"What is his name?" asked Petey.

"Sergeant Stuffy," replied Goggles, "and I must warn you, he is a little weird."

5
Stuffy Shares Lucky's Luck

After some breakfast feeding, Goggles and Petey headed to the north shore in search of answers and a way to pass boredom. It did not take long for Goggles to find his old friend. As Goggles and Petey got close to the bank, the bushes exploded and a brown streak of fur waddled furiously toward the water. Sergeant Stuffy was armed with a stick sharpened at one end and the most determined look ever seen on a gopher. During his mad dash at the birds he shouted a barely understandable, "Who is approaching my bank!"

As the final words from his question rang out, he fell into one of the many holes he dug around the pond bank. The sight of Stuffy tripping into his hole and breaking his trusty stick brought smiles and head shaking from the intruders.

"It's me!" shouted Goggles.

Trying to dislodge his foot, Stuffy replied, "I know a lot of animals, none named 'me', give your name or be prepared for trouble."

Goggles whispered to Petey, "I told you he was a little weird."

As Stuffy got closer, Petey could see that his face was all caked in mud and he had tiny leaves and twigs tied to his body for camouflage. An old combat helmet was perched crooked on top of his head. His expression was one of eagerness but frustration as his foot was stuck in a hole.

It's Goggles," shouted Goggles.

'Gobbles', Stuffy asked himself. "Ah yes, Gobbles, so good to see you," replied the Sergeant. "And who is this with you?"

Goggles looked at Petey and shrugged. "It is my friend; may we come up the bank?"

"Certainly," replied the rodent.

As Goggles and Petey climbed the bank, Stuffy became dislodged. Extending a hand to Petey, he tripped into another hole and slammed headlong, into Peteys' belly.

Not missing a beat or offering an apology, Stuffy stood up and welcomed his visitors to his hill. "How are you?," asked Stuffy to Goggles.

"I am doing well; we are here for a day and I wanted to check in to say hi. That was quite a fireworks display last night," suggested Goggles.

"Budgeawinkle, it is the same old stuff, I am just sick of it," replied Stuffy. "Hey," he added, "has anyone seen my spear?"

Petey started to point at the broken shaft along Stuffy's ambush path but Goggles gave him a quick look. Goggles spoke up, "You must have left it in your hole."

"Right, Right," said Stuffy, "somewhere in there. So boys, what is new in the big world of migratories?"

Goggles exchanged stories and small talk about his year gone by, including how he met Petey and the rest of it. Stuffy spent time discussing his year and all the "intruders" who have happened up on his bank. Petey listened to the stories with amusement, especially every time Stuffy referred to Goggles as Gobbles. Petey could see by Goggles face it was not funny to him-which made it funnier for Petey.

Finally Stuffy said, "Gobbles, have you run into any old friends?"

As Goggles started to reply, Petey quickly spoke up. He explained the story about what happened that morning and how the young duck seemed out of place. As soon as Petey mentioned duck, Stuffy spoke up.

"Hold it, hold everything, you are talking about Lucky. Was he a mallard duck?"

"Yes he was," said Petey.

"Yes, I know him well, though I have not seen him in a few weeks," added Stuffy.

"I was just wondering," asked Petey, "why is he so angry and mean?"

"Let me tell you about Lucky," said Stuffy, "but first I must say…I told them it was going to be a big one."

Petey and Goggles looked at each other and Goggles rolled his eyes.

"I was training, preparing for any incoming air assaults and I noticed the skies were getting darker. I can sense trouble -it comes from always being alert," Stuffy continued, "My eyes spotted the trouble before it hit and I decided to tell the rest of the pond. I ran around the pond and told all the animals that a big storm was coming; some listened because they felt the same thing. Others just kept on their way. When that duck family swam by, I ran down the hill and told them what was happening. Father Duck in his proper way said, "thanks" and paddled away without so much as a hint of concern. Well, Petey and Gobbles," Stuffy paused for effect, "it was the biggest hurricane to ever hit this area- Hurricane Frances. Even Mouse Land was quiet. Our whole pond was different, I woke up to holes on my hill that I never saw before- all from the pouring rain. "Wait a second," the sergeant stopped his story and stared at Petey. "Aren't you a pelican?" he asked.

"Why, yes," said Petey, stunned by the abrupt halt to his story.

Sergeant shrugged to himself and continued right where he left off. "When the skies cleared, we set out on foot patrol to check the enemy damage. The damage was complete, whole families were now refugees struggling to piece together their homes. The looks on my friend's faces brought me back to the big wars. There was one tiny miracle; Buster was touring collateral damage on the south quadrant when he decided to grab a milk container to help the fox family bail out their hole. When he got closer, he noticed a duck bobbing around inside the plastic jug. Buster, being a dim-witted beaver, brought the jug to me. Sure enough, if you wipe off all the mud, let him dry in the sun and wake him up- you have yourself a genuine mallard duck duckling. We named him Lucky, and you are right- he is one ornery duckling, but now you know why."

Petey and Goggles were staring at Stuffy in disbelief. There was no way they were prepared to hear that story. As they looked back at Stuffy, his eyes grew huge, his body tensed and in an instant he ran full speed to a large hole ten feet away. Diving into mid air, he landed two feet short of the hole and drove mud up into his nostrils and around his mouth. Scrambling to his feet, he reached the hole and fell down into it so all you saw was his back feet.

Goggles looked at Petey and repeated, "I told you he was different." After a few seconds, Stuffy came back out of his hole with mud in his mouth and all over his face.

As though nothing had just happened, Stuffy spoke again, "Hey, I tried to make him a recruit but he is too stubborn. Always troubling me, "Why?" "I'm tired," or his favorite- "you're not my Dad, you can't make me," finally I said 'forget it, go be a rush bum.' And that is where you saw him, in the rushes."

Everyone was quiet. Petey and Goggles were processing all that was said. Finally Goggles spoke up,

"Wow, you mean he has no parents?"

"That's right Gobbles," said Stuffy. Goggles winced. "He is on his own. No one in his family survived."

"I guess I understand his bitterness," said Petey, "he must be lonely, and scared."

"Every soldier has a friend on this pond if he wants one. The problem with Lucky is, well, he doesn't know how lucky he is."

6
Birds of a Feather

Petey and Goggles ate their way back to the flock in silence. Goggles was still steaming about the Gobbles thing. This is the part Petey hated about himself. He cannot let go of thinking. Most Pelicans would eat, get a full belly, and sleep. But not Petey; he wanted to help Lucky. But how? He didn't even know him... plus, Lucky certainly didn't seem to like Petey much at all.

Just then a rock landed six inches from Petey's head and splashed in the pond. Petey jumped into the air instinctively and then wondered what the heck just happened. Looking over his shoulder he saw Lucky rocking back and forth in the water, laughing heartedly. Petey swung his flight around and splashed right in front of Lucky.

"What's the big idea, startling me like that?"

"We're even," shouted Lucky, "I'm just paying you back for your scaring me this morning."

A smile slowly appeared on Petey face, "Okay, fine, we are even."

Lucky stared back, "I just want you to know that I don't like being even, I like being one up."

Petey shook his head. "What has a duck like you been doing all day?" asked Petey.

"Chasing the baby alligators; you have to harass them while you can. If you're quick, you can get a ride on their back," said Lucky with a smug look.

"You better not get caught by the mother, she will stuff her pillow with you."

"I told you, I am not afraid of anything, including some overgrown smelly luggage bag."

"Do you have to call everyone names?" asked Goggles.

"Listen you long necked, black beaked poop machine, as a matter of fact I do- Gobbles!"

"Hey, where did you get my name, and that is not my name. Wait a second, were you spying on us?!"

"I do not have time for spying." With that, Lucky jumped into the air and flew off into the swamp.

Goggles was furious, "Who does he think he is? That snotty little duck!"

Petey stopped him, "Goggles, you need to look at things from his point of view, maybe this is his way of reaching out to someone. Maybe he doesn't know the proper way to act- he certainly would not learn it from Sergeant Stuffy."

"I guess," said Goggles, "but he better learn soon or someone will make duck stew out of him."

Petey thought to himself, I think I know some birds that could teach him.

As the sun lowered, the evening feeding began. The flock moved along the shallows feeding on the tender grass roots and plants. Petey was the only bird that needed to be aloft to feed. He would make large arches above the flock looking for fish just under the water. When he spotted one, he would swoop down in the shape of an arrow and slam head first into the water. Often Petey would come up with nothing but a mouth and throat full of water. But when all worked out, he would have his fish. Most of the geese put up with the constant splashing as they grazed, but some did not. The leaders would come together and watch- two wore a disgusted look.

7
Petey's Generous Mistake

After the evening feeding, word spread throughout the flock that they would be moving in the morning. The leaders felt the winds would be favorable for a long flight. Petey was happy to hear they would be flying along the coastline. It was not that the fresh water fish tasted awful; they just needed more salt. Even though his bay was far behind, he still felt more comfortable with the smell of salt water around him. Fortunately, there were no frogs in his diet yet. During times of silence his thoughts went back to Lucky. He could not imagine life without his family and friends. Though he rarely saw his parents, they taught him all the important things in life like how to appreciate the natural beauty in things, rules of being a safe pelican and how to be a good friend. As far as not having friends, well, Petey just could not imagine that! The gang back in Tampa Bay is everything to him. Without friends, whom would you fish with? Whom would you play with? Whom would you hang out with? Petey just could not fathom that either. As he thought about these things, he realized what he must do.

"Hey Goggles, I will be right back."

"Where are you going?," he yelled after Petey. "I'm going to the rushes; don't worry I'll be back before dark."

"You're crazy, do you know what the rushes are like at night?"

Petey flew out over the lake and circled north to the rushes. He did not know how to say it, but he knew what he needed to say. With a big splash, he landed just outside the rushes.

With the sky growing darker, the rushes looked very different. Petey got a very uncomfortable feeling as he began to paddle in. Looking over his shoulder he could no longer see the lake behind him. Like a black curtain, this part of the swamp was sheltered from the rest. Petey wondered how a place could be so different without light. Even the smells seemed different. The smell of decay and rot were everywhere. A cloud of hungry mosquitoes took turns trying to penetrate Petey's outer feathers as he explored the ever-darkening swamp. The deeper Petey paddled, the spookier it got. Finally, he thought, 'I need to talk to Lucky and get the heck out of here; this place is creepy.'

"Lucky," he quietly stammered. "Lucky, are you here?"

Petey heard something slip off the bank and land in the water.

"Lucky," he shouted a little louder, "Lucky where are you?"

Again, a slight splashing and the far off hoot of an owl broke the silence. Petey could feel the sensation of night creatures moving silently all around him. His heart began to race. Wanting to call for Lucky, Petey only could sit silently hoping he could sense his surroundings. The sky grew darker, as silence continued to answer. He felt his dinner begin to rise in his flappy throat. Suddenly he felt a tug on his foot! Instinctively he jumped into the air. Just as Petey felt the sensation of flight bringing him to safety, he was hit from behind. It felt like a full size pier hit him square on the back of the head. Petey tumbled down, out of control into the water. His vision was gone, a high ringing filled his ears, and the world disappeared as he blacked out.

When Petey opened his eyes, it only confused him more. Large colorful flowers of fire were exploding over his head. The sky was alive with beams of light as bright as the sun. Back and forth they went; Petey thought he was still dreaming. He felt the sensation of moving. As his head cleared, he looked over his shoulder and saw the back of a duck pulling him through the water.

"Lucky?" he spoke. Lucky stopped swimming and spun around quickly. Petey tried to sit up in the water, his head hurt like crazy.

"Well, how are you doing Petey?"

"My head hurts, what happened?"

"I said how are you doing?"

"Okay, I guess, but my head hurts." Just then Lucky swooped up and slapped Petey right in his head. "You almost got us killed you stupid Salty!" quacked Lucky.

Petey, not expecting the slap, felt his head explode in pain.

"Ouch, you crazy duck, what the heck are you doing?"

"Do you know how close you came to having your last seafood dinner you dumb pelican?"

As the fire began to leave his head, Petey looked at Lucky, and he could tell by the anger in his eyes that he screwed up.

"What happened? What did I do?," asked Petey.

Lucky turned to face Petey.

"Petey, never ever go in the rushes. I heard you calling my name and I came to get you out of there. As I came around the corner, I saw you hop out of the water as that hawk hit you in the back of the head. The hawk is from the third pond up; he is always coming into our turf. When you got into the air, he hit you from behind. I jumped on him as you hit the water and I think that shocked him."

Lucky held out his wing "Do you see these?," he continued.

"What are those?" asked Petey.

"These are his left flight feathers, if you see a hawk flying in circles, he is the one that messed with you. I'm bringing you back to the flock where you will be safe."

Petey managed a "thanks" as his fog slowly lifted.

As the pair paddled toward the flock, Lucky turned to Petey, "Why were you in the rushes in the first place?"

In all the confusion, Petey forgot his mission. "Oh yeah, we are flying out in the morning, would you like to join us?"

Lucky scoffed, "That's it, that is why you almost got killed- boy what a pea brain. Do you think I would fly with a stuck up, right-to-do, fancy pants, look-down-their-nose flock like yours?... fat chance of that! I told you, I do not need anybody. You guys come around here looking to spread sympathy and walk off feeling great about yourself. Leave me out of it. I'll see you later."

Lucky began his trademark leaving the scene.

"Wait!" shouted Petey, and with that his head throbbed. Lucky turned to face him.

Petey continued, "I went into the rushes because I wanted you to fly with us. All you ever do is complain, call everyone names and announce how you do not need anyone. Some day nobody will ask you. If you want to keep stomping off and hanging out in the rushes, then so be it. I don't have sympathy for you; I am just giving you a choice. Goggles and I are enjoying our travels and I thought you might too. If you don't then, so be it; now, it is my turn to stomp off- we leave at sunrise if you change your mind!" Petey swam away, his head hurting from the shouting.

Goggles swam up to Petey as he entered the sleeping flock and whispered. "Why did you go to the rushes, are you crazy?"

"Yes, I guess I was, and I have a headache to prove it. I went to ask Lucky to join us."

"Are you nuts?" replied Goggles in a shouting whisper. "My Uncle will kill us if he comes along. The leaders are already annoyed by you, can you imagine them if Lucky showed up?"

"Well, don't worry," Petey whispered back, "he won't show up anyway."

Petey never thought about what the leaders would think. His head hurt badly, but not bad enough to keep him from falling asleep quickly.

8
On the Move Again

Petey awoke to the noisy assembling of order for the long flight. Again it started slowly. The geese would make lots of honking and splashing; they would jump to the air and circle the pond many times. With the deep blues and hints of orange in the sky, Petey could not help but enjoy the sight of his flock dancing on the morning air currents. His head felt slightly better, but he knew he was in for a long flight. He could not wait to see the coastline again; all this fresh water and last night's drama gave him the feeling that he would not miss this place.

Goggles swam over and said, "Are you ready?"

"Can't wait, lets get out of here."

"Follow me," said Goggles.

Petey jumped to the air and pumped hard. His muscles were sore from the tumble, but the flight brought a feeling of exhilaration and comfort.

The gift of flight was something Petey never took for granted. He remembers his mother returning to the nest with breakfast in her mouth for him. He would watch her leave and wish so bad to follow. When the day came to join her, Petey would never be the same. Flight is soft. With all that is rough in the world, flight is soft. The air feels like a fluffy pillow gently lifting you up and bringing you wherever you would like to go. The view from above brings understanding to all below. What seems so confusing with many questions on the ground, makes total sense when aloft. Petey always appreciated that; he had enough questions as it was.

Again, from nowhere the V started to form. Petey got right up next to Goggles and matched wing strokes. As the flock circled the pond one more time, Goggles looked at Petey and pointed down to the far bank. There he saw old Sergeant Stuffy running for cover behind one of his bunkers. In his mad dash for cover, he stepped into another hole and fell just short of the bunker sending his helmet bouncing down the hill into the water. Petey looked at Goggles smiling and said "Did you see that Gobbles?" Goggles shot Petey a look, then a grin crossed his face.

The flock flew on for most of the morning without incident; the leaders were wise to have waited because the wind was favorable for easy flight. Around noon, the flock could see the coastline. Petey could see a huge circle with bright colored cars traveling on it. People were crowded watching them go around and around. Petey wondered out loud to Goggles why they were doing that; Goggles replied, "You sure are a curious Pelican."

Seeing the salt water made Petey feel good, his headache was mostly gone. He never thought that a hawk would attack him like that; he would never forget it.

The flock continued to fly throughout sunset deep into the night. The leaders felt they had the strength to take advantage of the air currents. When they finally landed, it was dark and all were tired. They picked a river called the Altamaha River to rest. The water was slow and lazy with thick Spanish moss hanging to the waterline. The sight of the shoreline swamps made Petey uneasy. He was sure to stay clear of the shoreline and out in open water. The flock settled itself for sleep very quickly and all was quiet.

Morning came to more of the same. The flock had an early start. Petey was beginning to enjoy the routine of travel. The flock passed a number of beautiful sites on the third day. Flying over Savannah and seeing the beautiful brick-lined streets, passing over Hilton Head and Edisto Island. But what Petey will always remember is a sight off the coast of Charleston. The water was filled with sailboats of every color. Petey wanted to swoop down to take a closer look, but he remembered the warnings of leaving the V. The sailboats were everywhere. The sight of so many colors over the deep blue water with a clean frothy white wake behind them will always be in his mind. This would be something to share with Horace. Petey thought about his friend; he hoped he was doing well.

The day went quickly, darkness settled as the flock took up their night-time home. This was a small pond behind a park full of bright lights in Myrtle Beach. By the sounds of the night, people thrilled at the fast-moving trains they rode and the spinning rides they were on. By mid-night, Petey was sick of the noise and yearned for the peace and quiet of last night. Unfortunately for him, he could not sleep. The flock seemed to sleep just fine, but here was Petey, wide-awake and thinking. Suddenly, off at the far end of the pond he heard a loud splash. Petey looked up to see what made it. Nobody else seemed to move. Paddling passed a sleeping Goggles, Petey moved closer. All the lights from shore were shutting down, so the darkness was getting more complete. Petey stopped at the end of the flock and peered into the growing darkness; he heard nothing. Maybe I am imagining, he thought in his head. Then he saw it, way at the end of the pond, the dark shape of something on the water. As Petey approached, he had the remaining light at his back, making it very hard for the lone figure to see him, but he could see out just fine.

Petey paddled up close "How do you do?" said Petey.

The shape turned around with huge eyes and started to fly away. Petey thought, "Lucky."

"Lucky, is that you?" he called after him. Petey smiled to himself, it sure was; Lucky was here on the pond! Petey decided to wait. Before long, his wait paid off. Lucky swooped in and landed next to Petey.

"Hey old friend, how did you get here?" Lucky did not say anything.

"What's wrong?" asked Petey. Lucky still did not say anything. Petey sensed Lucky was embarrassed, so he backed off.

They both sat in silence for a moment, then Lucky finally spoke. "After you left, I was worried because of how you know nothing about safety-especially in the rushes. I thought I would watch to see how you were doing and if you needed help I could help you. So I decided to follow you. But I see you are doing well so I will be heading back now."

Petey spoke in a matter of fact tone. "I understand, makes perfect sense, how about sleeping with us tonight and heading out in the morning?"

"If you insist," said Lucky. "I suppose just for tonight." They paddled together back to the flock.

Goggles was surprised to see Lucky in the morning. His facial expressions indicated his displeasure with Lucky's return. Petey noted this and gave Goggles space. One thing about Goggles that Petey learned a long time ago, it takes a while for Goggles to warm up to you. After morning feeding an unusual occurrence happened. The leaders called a flock meeting. All the flock gathered together in perfect straight lines. When the leaders spoke, everyone was still and quiet.

Goggle's Uncle spoke first. "Good morning flock, we have called this meeting to tell you we are flying straight through to the Chesapeake Bay. We may have to fly straight through the night as the winds are perfect. Eat a hearty breakfast, be ready to fly. As always, we will talk to you down the line if we have anything to say. Remember, there are plenty of dangers in the Bay; the hawks live under every bridge. Keep a keen eye out, we will sleep two days from now."

The other leader added, "Keep the V tight and do not fall behind; I hope you heard what was said- be aware of the hawks under the bridge!"

Petey could not help think, "Sure, now you tell me."

With that, the meeting broke up. Nobody said a word to the leaders; the flock disbursed and began feeding again.

Petey paddled up to Goggles, "So, do you think Lucky can join us?"

"I told you before Petey, it is not a good idea."

"We can't just leave him here, can we?"

"I don't have an answer. Look Petey, you are my friend. I wanted you to join us to experience all the sights of travel. I knew you were strong enough and I knew you would follow the rules. You have shown respect for my flock and you are a great travel companion. But ever since you met Lucky, you have been away from the flock and all wrapped up in helping him. You heard Sergeant Stuffy, Lucky does not listen. If he does that with the flock, they will kick him out of the V- and possibly you too. Now I know you are trying to help, but you have to be on your own with this one. I have no idea what the flock will think."

"Thanks for your concern Goggles," said Petey, "I understand what you are saying. I will have to think about it- the thing is Lucky never had ANYBODY. Don't you think he deserves a shot?"

"Yes I do, just not now, not with this flock," answered Goggles, as he paddled away.

Goggles was right, the flock would be upset and Petey knew that Lucky would not follow the rules. But still, he wanted to risk it. If Lucky took off the same time as he did and stayed between him and Goggles, what kind of trouble would there be?

He approached Lucky, "Well, are you going to travel with us or not?"

"Sure," answered Lucky, "you guys may need some help staying out of trouble."

"Great," said Petey, "here is what you need to do."

Petey went through all the flock rules and routines. Lucky sat listening; he commented only to say, "That is stupid," when Petey spoke of not talking to the leaders.

"Stupid or not, those are the flock rules- do you understand?"

"Sure," said Lucky, "I got it."

9
The Leaders Speak

After morning feeding the leaders jumped into the air, which summoned the rest of the flock to come together. The flock was setting out on its longest, continuous flight, and Petey was happy for it. The park next to their pond was filling with people. One boy was throwing bread to the seagulls near the beach. Petey thought to himself, "Silly Salties."

As the V began to form, Petey told Lucky to get in front of him and behind Goggles. Lucky had a strong wing beat; he had no problem matching the speed and rhythms of the flock. They flew all morning crossing over the beautiful Cape Fear with seabirds that Petey had never seen. The many causeways, bridges and islands reminded Petey of Bradenton and Sarasota.

The flock moved along swiftly and without incident. As the flock rounded Cape Lookout to head out into the Pamlico Sound, a leader looked back. Petey saw his eyes, and so did Goggles. The leader immediately spoke to the one next to him, who in turn spoke to Goggles' uncle. They flew along for some time, and then the first leader said something to the goose behind him. That goose turned and spoke to the one behind him. This continued for some time; the flock showed increasing discomfort. With each passing of the message, more concerned faces appeared. The message finally reached Goggles. Petey held his breath, hoping his instinct was wrong.

When Goggles finally turned to face Petey, Petey knew. In Goggles' eyes he saw a tear form; his face indicated helplessness and sadness. Goggles could not speak the message; he opened his beak to speak and only managed to shake his head as more tears welled up in his eyes. Petey saw his friend's emotions and he looked at Lucky. Lucky was confused, "What's the problem Petey?" Petey looked at Lucky and said, "Follow me, you and I are out of the V."

Petey banked quickly to his right and down. Lucky shrugged his shoulders and followed. Pulling up alongside Petey Lucky shouted "It's a lot harder outside the V, can't we get back in line?"

"No," replied Petey, "they kicked us out, we are on our own."

"They can't do that!" shouted Lucky, "Who do they think they are?" Petey did not reply.

Lucky shouted, "I'll fix this, they cannot do this to my friend." With that Lucky took off. Petey saw this and immediately followed.

Catching up with Lucky he grabbed the duck from behind and pulled him back, "Don't!" he shouted, "You will make it worse for Goggles. Drop it Lucky, it's over, leave it alone!"

Lucky stopped and matched Petey's flight speed. They flew together behind the flock watching it get further and further away. Lucky did not know what to say, so he said nothing. Petey's mind was going crazy; how could he be so stupid? He should have listened to Goggles. Now everything was over. He could never find Surprise on his own. He won't see Goggles until next winter, if ever. He felt like banging his head on something. Why did he let this happen? The sense of frustration and failure overwhelmed Petey as tears welled in his eyes.

The flock had all but disappeared when Lucky spoke up. "Hey, what's that?"

Petey squinted into the distance, trying to see what Lucky was speaking of.

"I don't see anything."

"That's because you have eyes like a scrawny bat," remarked Lucky, "something flew away from the V."

Petey continued to stare and sure enough Lucky was right. One of the geese had pealed off the V and was heading in their direction.

"Maybe they have come to invite us back," said Petey.

"I wouldn't go if they asked," replied Lucky. Petey shot him a disgusted look. As the shape grew closer, Petey saw who it was. After making a large arch in the sky, Goggles found himself gliding alongside his old friend Petey.

"Hey Petey," Goggles said with more questions in his voice than solutions.

Petey looked at Goggles in astonishment. "What are you doing here?" asked Petey.

"I thought for sometime and felt that if the V would not let you fly with them, then I would not fly with the V."

"Good for you," piped in Lucky, "who needs them?"

Goggles looked silently at Lucky and his face began to twist into rage. No longer able to control his emotions he shouted, "That's my family, don't talk about them like that! You do not know the first thing about them! That's why we are in this mess to begin with, you have NO RESPECT!"

Goggles shouted so loud one could hear the frustration leaving his body. Lucky was obviously surprised by the verbal attack; he began to speak to defend himself but changed his mind. Making a sweeping arch, he banked to his left and flew off. Petey was astonished; he did not know what to say. The two flew for several minutes in silence. Finally Goggles spoke up, "He will be back Petey, you mean too much to him. I am sorry I lost it back there."

"It has been a tough day for all of us," said Petey.

"Look at the bright side Petey, we can still see the flock, and we are keeping up."

"I agree, but can we do this forever? I mean, this is hard work."

"When we get to the Chesapeake Bay, I will approach my uncle. I know you are not allowed to do that, but it is our only hope. What is the worst he can do, we are already kicked out of the V."

They flew along together for the rest of the afternoon. As the sun began to set, they were over Albermarle Sound. The beautiful colors and gentle shoreline brought Petey away from his current situation. He was watching all the boats returning from fishing the Outer Banks, with bands of seagulls that resembled a parachute pulled behind each watercraft. Petey thought of his friend, the fisherman, on his pier at Bradenton Beach. He wondered if he ever fished here at the Outer Banks. He kind of missed his friends a little. When things are going well, it seems like you never appreciate the friends in your life. But when times are tough, is when friends are needed the most. Here Petey was, thinking about the gang. What would they do? He knew what they would do; they would be there for each other. They would never abandon each other like Lucky did. He stole a glance at Goggles gliding along next to him and thought about what he did for Petey. He left his friends and family in the V to fly along side of him. Petey would never forget that. Goggles was a good friend.

Petey's daydreaming came to an instant end as a green blur slammed into his right wing. In an awkward display of affection, Lucky slammed into Petey and announced a quick, curt "I'm sorry."

Petey looked at Goggles then back at Lucky, "he is the one you need to talk to." Lucky swooped over and pulled up alongside Goggles. "Sorry about what I said, I will try not to screw up anymore." Lucky said in a low voice.

"It's okay," replied Goggles, "I'm sorry I lost my temper."

The three flew along for a long time without speaking. With the flock not stopping, they knew they could not. After a while, without even doing it intentionally, they formed a V, with Goggles in the lead.

10

V For Victory

Throughout the night, the new V had no idea whether the flock was ahead of them or not. Occasionally the wind would bring the soft sounds of honking, and then they would hear nothing for hours at a time. After many hours of guessing their route, finally the sun began to peer over the Atlantic. The first rays of light increased the lead flock's noise, much to the relief of the small V. As the light grew, Petey was stunned by what he saw. Stretched out in front of him was the most breathtaking view of a bay that Petey ever saw. With stunned silence, all he could do was glide. The leaders were right, bridges, beautiful bridges spanned across the deep blue waters. The growing light painted the sky with reds and gold. The twinkling cars moved in unison over a bridge so low that the cars appeared to drive on the water. The whole bay seemed alive with boats and cars.

Petey finally managed a word, "Wow," he said toward Goggles.

Goggles smiled, "I knew you would like this part Petey."

"I have never seen such a busy piece of water; it's so alive," said Petey.

Goggles looked at Lucky, "Wait until this Salty sees New York Harbor."

"Is this the Chesapeake Bay, Goggles?"

"Yes Lucky, it looks like we chose the right route; there is the flock down below us. Be sure to keep an eye on where they land, if they do."

As the three passed over the Chesapeake Bay Bridge, Petey noted that they were leaving the Atlantic.

"Are we leaving the coastline Goggles?"

"Yes, we will be inland for a while now; don't worry, there is plenty of salt water. The bay is very big, and full of food. We stop here every year. I wouldn't be surprised if my uncle brings the flock down by the Seagull Fishing Pier. It is right up ahead."

Just as if on cue, the flock began to circle. Slowly, one by one, the V settled down next to the many bridges and piers jutting out into the bay. Goggles turned to Lucky and Petey and said, "We know where they are; let's get some distance away and set down ourselves; I don't know about you guys, but I am pooped."

They both nodded and headed to a small pier within sight of the flock.

After landing, the group paddled together. Goggles spoke first. "I do not want to alarm either one of you, but remember what the leaders said in Myrtle Beach; this bay is full of hawks. Do you see all these piers and bridges?," said Goggles waving his wing around. "Under every one is a hawk, and if he is hungry, we better be alert to him."

"I am not afraid of no stupid hawk," said Lucky, "tell him what I did to that hawk that tried to hurt you Petey. Oh wait, you can't because you slept through the whole thing."

"I wasn't asleep- oh forget it," said Petey. Sometimes Lucky was not worth arguing with.

"Well Lucky, if you are not afraid, that's fine, but for our sake let's stick together and keep a close eye out," suggested Goggles. "One should be awake while the others sleep; you two rest now and I will sleep later."

Petey did not argue with that one; he was asleep in the shade of the fishing pier while listening to the gentle lapping of the bay's water.

11
Small V...Big Victory

"I say old chap, it is thirty feet high."

"I beg to differ, it's at least fifty."

"Is that during maximum draw of the moon or minimum moon draw?"

"You know it is the mean quotient of the tide, didn't you pay attention in school? You always take the mean quotient on this bay; they teach that to you the first day."

"I am well aware of that, but the mean is not always the correct response based on the inquiry."

"Do you see, there you go, that is why you are not an intellectual challenge any more; you over think every question."

"I'm not a challenge? Listen academic simpleton, I know more than you in just my medulla."

"The medulla is not where you think, dolt."

"Precisely, your catching on, would you like me to present you with a theorem for every sarcastic remark I make?"

"I will give you a theorem. If A = Gorry and B= truth then A plus B equals ignoramus."

"Oh yeah, the square root of Rasty equals a fish-breathed, loud mouth with the brain power of a goat."

Petey, startled from his sleep, shouted out to the otters, "Will you two, whoever you are, stop bickering?"

The two river otters spun around, to face the voice. They looked at each other and slipped under the water. Petey looked around, smiled to himself, hoping they would pop up again. He was not disappointed; up they popped right next to him.

"Hi," said Petey to the two otters.

The otters looked at each other, then back at Petey, then back to each other. Finally one spoke, "He is always in dissent," the one said to Petey, "I've told him hundreds of times, he is wasting oxygen and contributing to global warming with all his hot air."

"You are the one who begins it every time," replied the other. "Your vexing prattle leads to my displeasure."

"Wait, wait, wait, can you two stop for a second?!" said Petey in frustration. "First of all, I can't understand a word you are saying, you use too big of words."

The two otters looked at each other and cocked their heads back to Petey.

Petey continued, "If you would stop and be silent, I would like to introduce myself. My name is Petey."

The two otters smiled at each other and shook Petey's wing. The first otter started to speak and Petey cut him off. "Wait, now remember, be nice."

"Hi, said the otter haltingly, "My name is Gorry, this is my brother, Rasty."

"It is nice to meet you both," said Petey, "do you live here?"

"Yes, well sort of, we live over on the shore; we come out here to get some free meals from the fisherman on the pier," said Rasty. "We were just verbalizing our estimate on the vertical height of the piers sub-structure."

Petey looked at Rasty, "Say what?" asked Petey "There you go again, normal words please."

Gorry spoke up, "Bozo here thinks that pylon is thirty feet high; I say fifty."

"That's better, but try not to call him names," said Petey, "anyway, why do you care?"

"Well," said Rasty, "that is part of our assignment of the day."

Petey looked befuddled.

Rasty continued, "Every day we swim into the bay and analyze some part of it. That is how you keep your mind sharp. We have discovered a wealth of important knowledge. Did you know the underwater migration routes of the blue crab during the last lunar phase in August? Thought not. How about the refractory angles of the summer solstice sun during low tide?"

Petey just shook his head in disbelief.

Gorry elbowed Rasty, "That is enough, will you pipe down know-it-all".

Rasty started to return comment when Petey spoke up. "Have you seen any of my friends?"

"What do they look like?"

"One is a goose and one is a duck."

"Oh, I think so, follow me."

Petey followed the two otters around the pier and looked out into the bay. What he saw took his breath away. In front of him had to be the largest flock of geese ever witnessed. There in the evening light were thousands of geese, maybe hundreds of thousands, all spread out in front of him.

"Are any of them your comrade?" asked Gorry.

Petey barely spoke, "I have no idea," still in awe.

Just then a splash landed right behind Petey "Hey sleepy head, look who's up."

Petey did not remove his eyes from the geese. "Hey Lucky, where did all these geese come from?" Petey asked still staring.

"I have no idea, they were here when I woke up."

"Where is Goggles?" asked the distracted pelican.

"When I woke up, he said he would be back after he got some shuteye, I was up on the pier waiting for you to wake up. Who are your friends?"

"Oh sorry," Petey broke out of his trance, "this is Rasty and Gorry; they are brothers."

"Hi," the otters said in unison.

Lucky looked back, "Is it true that otters are always playing?"

The two otters looked at each other "Indubitably," said Rasty.

"I'll bet you know a lot of jokes to pull," smiled Lucky.

"You've come to the correct vicinage."

"What?" asked Lucky.

"He means 'yes we do,'" said Gorry.

Lucky smiled widely, "Come with me, we have to talk," summoning his new found friends to come with him.

They paddled away to a quiet spot and all wore mischievous smiles.

Petey turned his attention back to the flock spread out before him; how the heck would they find their flock in all those geese, he wondered.

"Hey Petey," Petey heard a voice say. Whirling around he saw nothing.

"Up here," the voice said again. Petey looked up and saw his buddy.

"Hey Goggles, what are you doing up there?"

"Just walking the pier. A fisherman gave me some pretzel rods so I am just walking to see if anything is left over. Come on up."

Petey jumped out of the water and with a few wing pumps was sitting by his friend looking out over the water. "I never imagined there could be so many geese," said Petey.

"You know, most are related to me; it's a big family. All Atlantic Flyway geese come through here at some point. It is probably the biggest gathering in the world. I have been talking to many throughout the day. It is like a yearly reunion. It's always good seeing old friends. Many heard about me getting kicked out of the V. Word spread quickly with all these cackling honkers."

"Do you know where our flock is?" asked Petey.

"Yeah, they were just up the bay a little last I checked. They will not go too far."

"Let's go for a walk," suggested Petey, "I am starving."

They walked up the pier looking for food. Goggles was happy to find some left over potato chips lying on the pier; Petey gorged on bait buckets left unattended. It didn't take long and the two friends were stuffed. They sat with full bellies quietly enjoying the view of the bay in the disappearing light. Not really focused on anything they both took in the sights.

In the life of a traveling pelican and a goose, a full belly, a good conversation and a friendship is a lot. Both Goggles and Petey were enjoying the moment.

Just then Petey and Goggles saw a shape dart by out of the corner of their eyes, then another. The shape resembled a flying "M".

"Did you see that?" asked Petey.

"Yes I did," replied Goggles quietly, "do not move and be silent."

Petey and Goggles sat solitary looking down on the massive flock below. Both felt a sense of responsibility and concern. They then heard voices, a high-pitched voice that was spoken very low.

"There is one, he looks big enough for everyone," said one voice.

"He looks too strong, how about the little one next to him," said the other voice.

Petey's heart began to quicken as he sat silently. He was glad to be up on the pier, but what about all those geese below him- and Lucky was down there!

The voices continued, "This is really too easy."

"I know," replied the other, "I told you this is a great time of the year, geese everywhere, take your pick."

Petey stole a silent glance at Goggles. Goggle's words came back to him, 'most are related to me' was playing in his mind. Who was it that was talking? Were they the hawks that Petey had been warned about? Was there a way to stop them?

All these questions whirred around in Petey's head. Petey knew what to do to get answers, the same way he got most of his answers. He needed to get in the air, flight would solve everything. But…how could he do that without being detected?

Just then one spoke, "What about the duck?"

That was it, Petey looked at Goggles and jumped into the air as silent as he could. Flying as fast as he could he gained altitude. Looking down silently he could see Goggles where he left him; as far as he could tell nothing flew out from under the pier. Petey made a large arch around the pier while looking into the remaining bit of light for Lucky.

There he was, floating with Rasty, Gorry and a few geese just off the pier, almost directly below Goggles. Petey had to warn him of the danger, so he started to float down. As he came down toward his friend he saw the two flying "M"'s streak out from under the bridge toward one of the small geese in the flock. Without thinking, Petey went into a full feeding dive; wings tucked streaking toward the two hawks. The water was coming up fast, but Petey did not let up; full speed he hit the first hawk just as it arrived at the unsuspecting goose.

The impact of his dive slammed the hawk deep below the water. Petey felt his head hit the water with such a force that ringing filled his head and ears. He realized while underwater that the hawk was there too. The two were locked together for a brief second. Feathers, splashing, and commotion filled the air.

Goggles leapt off the pier and streaked toward the splashes. On Goggle's lead, the remaining geese in the small flock began to hiss and swim toward the fight. As the geese came together, the second hawk pulled out of his dive and began to fly up into the evening sky. As he began to turn, he was hit hard under his right wing by the very duck he was just looking at. Lucky hit the hawk with such force that he fell from the sky for twenty feet. Gathering himself he took off, never looking back.

Petey came to and pushed himself toward the surface. The hawk emerged at the same time. The crowd of geese, Petey's rage and the pain of the impact was enough for the hawk to make a quick exit. He jumped into the air, and started to rise. Again, a green streak hit the already dazed hawk. Lucky slammed the hawk hard toward the pier's pylon. The hawk narrowly escaped hitting the pylon. Gathering his flight and wits, he made a hasty exit toward the direction of his partner and flew off into the night.

"Are you alright?," asked Goggles.

Petey nodded his head, "I think so, just a little dizzy; did they hurt the small goose?"

"I don't know," replied Goggles.

"No, they didn't," said an unfamiliar voice. A proud mother goose was floating in front of Petey. "They didn't," she continued, "because of you and your friends' heroic actions. You three saved my daughter's life."

Petey became uncomfortable; he looked at Goggles. "We were in the right place at the right time ma'am, I am just glad she is okay."

Lucky landed next to Petey and Goggles. "That was awesome Petey!" he yelled. "I never saw anyone dive so fast."

Rasty and Gorry popped up. "Wow, that was stupendous!" they shouted together.

Petey spun toward Goggles. "Thanks buddy, thanks for joining in."

"Petey, that was the bravest thing I ever saw, I had no choice but to jump in. You're a crazy pelican."

"Those hawks didn't know what hit them," exclaimed Lucky, "that was great!"

By this time all the geese in the area had circled the six of them, Goggles, Petey, Lucky, the two otters and the mother goose were in the center of a huge circle of Atlantic Flyway geese. Over all the ruckus and honking, the mother goose turned and spoke directly to Goggles. "What flock are you from my lifelong friend?"

On the mother gooses' question, the whole flock grew silent.

Goggles did not know what to say; he remained silent as well.

The mother goose spoke again, "Do not be shy, please share with me your flock; I would like to speak to your leaders."

Goggles moved around uneasily not knowing what to say.

Petey spoke up, "You see, what Goggles is trying to say is-" Petey was cut off in his sentence. A loud voice called from the back of the flock.

"He is from our flock, flock of the Hudson Valley in Upstate New York!"

All the geese turned to look at the goose who spoke up. Goggles' uncle swam toward the center, looking upright, distinguished and very proud. He swam right up to Petey and Goggles.

"I have never been prouder of two in my flock," turning toward Lucky he corrected himself, "I mean three in my flock, than I am right now."

Goggles' uncle turned and faced the mother goose.

"We are their leaders," Goggles' uncle said to the mother goose.

Well, fine sir, may I speak directly to you?" asked the mother goose.

"You may speak to me," replied the leader.

"Thank you. I want to say that you should be very proud of these birds, though I must admit they are a different mix. I want to thank you for such fine leadership in guiding them. My flock of Green Pond, Northern New Jersey thanks you."

Goggles uncle lowered his head for a time, then raised it and looked at the three misfits in front of him and spoke.

"We leaders have made a terrible mistake; we judged our flock by their appearance and not by the content of their character."

He spoke slowly, pausing again, as if thinking as he spoke. "Goggles, you have made wise choices in the friends you spend time with. You have shown wisdom beyond your years. It is we, the leaders, who must learn that not all differences are bad. You bring strength to the flock with your differences, and we would be honored if you and your friends rejoin our V in the morning departure."

Goggles looked at his uncle. He opened his beak to talk and stopped. For ten seconds he sat silently, until finally his uncle smiled.

"I'm sorry, you have permission to speak to a leader."

Goggles grinned and spoke, "I speak for all three of us," he paused, "we would love to be with your V in the morning departure."

The three looked at each other and smiled. Petey felt an overwhelming sense of joy fill him.

12
Goggles' Gift of Travel

From the mouth of the Chesapeake Bay to Baltimore, was a day-long flight. The leaders decided not to go up the coastline. They felt the flock would cover more area flying passed Washington D.C. and into Baltimore. As they flew deeper into the Chesapeake, the shoreline was getting busier and busier. There was no such thing as a "peaceful" flight. Planes, boats, cars and buildings were everywhere. All this time, Petey flew along just soaking in all the sights. He thought back to the first time he met Goggles. Before meeting him, he always wondered about what was out there. It felt so good that flight was again answering some of those questions. The world was indeed beautiful.

The flock flew through one night and landed just outside Baltimore. Goggles excitedly called Petey and Lucky to follow him to the shoreline. Petey had no idea why, but he followed. Coming up to a building, Petey saw big glass windows.

Goggles spoke. "Hey you two, jump up on that pier and look in the windows."

Petey looked at Lucky and shrugged. He jumped out of the water and onto a pylon. Looking in the window, he was amazed at what he saw. It was a huge indoor swimming pool, with concrete seating all around it. Then he saw a dolphin leap clear out of the water and touch a big ball hanging from the ceiling. The crowd of people cheered as the dolphin performed some of the most amazing tricks Petey and Lucky had ever seen. The show ended, Petey and Lucky splashed down next to Goggles.

"What is this place?" asked Petey.

"It is an aquarium," said Goggles, "people come here to learn about our home. Isn't it funny, people want to learn about our home?"

Petey nodded, "Yeah, that is funny."

Petey thought, 'I guess I'm not the only one who wonders.'

13
Hopping Good Meal

Their stay in Baltimore was only one night. Following another flock meeting, it was announced they would fly straight through the night. They would be leaving the salt water and traveling over land for some time. Petey was sure to eat a good saltwater meal on his last feeding. The flock flew off at dawn; it was sprinkling a little during the morning, but cleared up shortly into the flight. The flock worked hard and covered a lot of ground. They flew over Wilmington, Philadelphia and Trenton. As they left Trenton, they took an unscheduled stop at Westhaven Farm near Allentown. They had to stop because of the rain.

Most of the flock did not complain; the field was full of grains and sweet grass. Even Lucky was content to mingle with the flock and feed with them. One of the members did complain.

"What the heck am I supposed to eat?" Petey asked Goggles.

Goggles shrugged. "The rain made us stop, what do you want me to do?"

"Find me something to eat," replied Petey.

Goggles continued eating and Petey sat sulking under a tree trying to stay dry.

As darkness settled, a funny thing started to happen. Goggles noticed it first. Little frogs began to hop out of the grass and across the muddy cornfield.

"Hey Petey," cried Goggles. "I found some food." Petey flew the short flight to Goggles. Petey looked down and sure enough there were frogs.

"You want me to eat them?"

"Sure, why not I have seen lots of fish eaters eat them."

Petey made a grimace and shrugged, "Here goes nothing."

He grabbed the frog and threw it back in his waddle. Goggles was staring at him, looking for his friend's reaction. Petey shook his head back and forth and swallowed.

"Well, what do you think?"

Petey did not answer immediately, sensing Goggles' anticipation was killing him. He licked his beak, shook his head, and rubbed his belly.

Finally he spoke

"Tastes like chicken."

The two broke out in laughter. There is something about mud and rain that makes you silly. They laughed for hours.

14
New York, New York

The rain stopped overnight. In the morning the flock was met with beautiful clear skies, though it was a little cooler. The tiny leaves just starting to come on the trees, and the sweet scent of the moist earth and the songs from the meadow birds- made for a wonderful wake up. Petey wondered to himself how much of 'where and how' you wake up affects how you feel during the day. He loved waking up by his pier in the bay, but he was sure enjoying all the new ways to wake.

All the frogs from the previous night were gone, so Petey would have to skip morning feeding. As the sun got higher, the flock gathered and took off. As they left the peaceful farm behind, Goggles turned to Petey and spoke, "I hope you enjoyed your day in the country because by nightfall you will be in the greatest city on the planet."

Petey called back, "Where are we going to next?"

"You will see."

The three flew all day, without much happening. Lucky had acquired some fishing line from his friends, Rasty and Gorry. He would sneak up behind some unsuspecting goose and gently tie a loop around his foot while he was distracted. Then Lucky would pull on the line, at which the goose would look around and wonder how he ended up outside the V.

Goggles learned to tolerate Lucky a lot more now. Though you could see he struggled with some of his goofiness. Lucky, for his part, just kept on being Lucky. He seemed to be a lot happier with the flock, and Petey could tell he was changing- for the better.

Late in the day Petey thought he saw water on the horizon. He was happy about that. When a pelican cannot see water, it is just not as comfortable. Sure enough, it was the ocean again, spread out before the flock. The leaders brought the flock lower as they approached the water. Petey did not understand this, but it did not take him long to realize why. A huge jet flew over the heads of the V, then another. Petey was shocked by the loud noise.

In a few more wing strokes, he saw it. There were no words to describe what was approaching into Petey's eyesight. In the late afternoon light, against a bright blue sky, the skyline of a huge city appeared. The leaders continued to bring the flock lower, Petey could see better now. Long Island stretched out in front of him: boats, bridges, cars, trucks, people and buildings were everywhere. The lights were starting to come on all around him. He was not sure, but there was a pulsating vibration in the air. The whole flock seemed alive and excited. Petey could not help feel very energetic and vibrant. Goggles turned and looked at Petey,

"What do you think?"

"And I thought Baltimore was busy; this must be New York City," Petey replied.

"Yes," said Goggles, "welcome to the greatest city on the planet. Welcome to New York!"

Petey flew for a long time not saying anything. He flew over the Varrazano Bridge, passing Brooklyn and into the Harbor. In front of him he saw the Statue of Liberty and the Brooklyn Bridge. An hour passed and the flock continued flying north. As the harbor turned into a river, Petey saw the Manhattan skyline all lit up. Further up the river he saw a massive baseball stadium. Just passed Yankee Stadium, the flock leaders brought the flock down. Petey splashed down and felt totally exhausted. The excitement had drained him. Goggles and Lucky paddled over to him.

"Wasn't that amazing?" asked Goggles, "the leaders timed it so we would see the lights coming on all over the city."

"I am speechless," replied Petey, "simply speechless."

The hustle and bustle of the harbor and roads all around them drew a strong contrast to anything Petey had ever experienced. He had never experienced anything so electric and alive. Their flight through New York Harbor was one Petey could not wait to share with Horace, though he knew his old friend could not imagine it.

15
April in the Spring

P etey awoke with the sounds of a soft conversation near him.

"Goggles, how much further until Surprise?" asked Lucky.

"When we leave the city, we will be flying up this river called the Hudson River. Some of the flock will start to leave as we go further up the river. We will leave the flock in about a day's flight."

"Will you be taking up a mate this season?"

"Yes, she will be meeting us up river near Coxsackie."

"What is her name?" asked Lucky.

"Her name is April," replied Goggles. "It is an easy name to remember because I see her every April."

"How many families have you had together?"

"Too many to count; we have known each other for a long time."

Petey paddled over to the two who had their back turned to him.

"What are you guys talking about?" Petey asked.

Goggles turned and faced his buddy, "I thought you were still sleeping."

"No, I'm up, what are you talking about?" Petey repeated more earnestly.

"Lucky was asking me about my plans for the summer, that's all."

"I heard you mention the name April, who is that?" asked Petey.

"She is Goggles' life mate," Lucky clarified, "all geese have a mate to have goslings with each Spring; Goggles mate's name is April."

Petey looked at Goggles, "You mean you are a dad?"

"Many times over Petey- many, many times," Goggles answered.

Petey smiled to himself, "Do you think you will have another family, this spring?" asked Petey.

"You can ask April when you see her," said Goggles.

Petey shook his head smiling broadly. "That is so cool- Goggles a dad- can't wait to see it. How much longer until the pond in Surprise?"

"Not far now Petey, we should be there in no time if we fly through. Today will be our last day with the leaders. We will meet them back here in the fall."

"You mean there will be no more V?" asked Petey

"That's right Petey, we will be on our own," replied Goggles.

"I love the V, and will miss the V, but I am looking forward to some free time," said Lucky.

Goggles looked at Lucky and started to say something and then stopped. Petey could sense the mixed feelings that Goggles was experiencing.

16
On Our Own Again

The flock took off up the river, around mid morning. The city peeled away behind them as the flock continued north. Following the river they passed the Tappan Zee Bridge. That bridge seemed like a line between the steel and lights of the city and the more tranquil setting found up river. Goggles was right, as they moved up the river more and more geese left the V. Often with little more than a glance and an occasional wink, they would swoop down and be on their own. Petey imagined that they would go to their own version of Goggles' Surprise Lake. 'What a joy traveling is,' Petey thought. When he started this trip, he never imagined the variety of ways of living. He met so many ways to live this life. He wondered if others appreciated the unique and exciting ways they live. He thought not. Most are like his friends at home; they just wake up every day, eat, sleep and do it all over again. Petey vowed never to stop appreciating life, big things and small things.

It was not long and the flock was down to very few. The leaders had all gone except Goggles' uncle. Being on the coastline for so long they had not seen mountains like the ones they were seeing now. The Catskills off in the distance and the steep cliffs on the waters edge brought new beauty to the scenery. Petey was truly feeling out of place, feeling more like a pelican pioneer than ever before. Without expecting it, Goggle's uncle pulled away from the lead and came back toward Goggles, Petey and Lucky. Speaking to the three, Goggle's uncle shouted over the wind "I will be leaving, have a great summer you three, I'll see you in the fall." The three looked back without replying, following proper etiquette. "In the fall, we have to do something about these stupid flock rules, be good!" he shouted as he dropped away from the flock.

The flock continued; some new leaders took over that Goggles did not recognize. Goggles turned to Petey, "Do you think we could do this on our own?"

"Been done before," Petey replied.

Goggles turned to Lucky and Petey and smiled, "We are out of here, follow me."

The three left the V and dropped closer to the water. With Goggles in the lead, the three flew forth on their own. Skimming just feet above the river, the three were positively excited. There is a special feeling that comes with being free, without any structure except what you want to do. The excitement in what might be and the power to control it is exhilarating. The three felt great.

The three flew along for a while and Goggles turned to Lucky.

"Would you like to take the lead?" asked Goggles.

Even Lucky was shocked. He never expected Goggles to ask that in a million years.

Lucky looked at Petey; Petey was smiling, and then he picked his head up nudging Lucky forward. Lucky flew along thinking for a second and before any warning, Goggles dropped low and ducked behind him. Before Lucky had a chance to make his decision, next thing he knew he was in the lead.

The day wore on and the three passed the Mid Hudson Bridge, then the Kingston Rhinecliff Bridge. Goggles shouted to Lucky to stop at the next Bridge. Lucky brought the three down outside of Catskill, NY at the Rip Van Winkle. The three settled down as the night had already fallen. Petey got his first look at a piece of ice floating down the river. It had bumped into him in the dark. Having never seen ice before, he followed it for some time before heading back to his friends.

17
Destination

Even though the early morning light shone down on him, Petey woke up because of the cold. It was very cold. No dim light was going to take this away. Cold was something that Petey was not used to. He shivered and felt very restless. With his friends still sleeping, he decided to take a flight. Not knowing where he was, the flight could not be long. Petey jumped into the air and circled the islands below the bridge. He already felt better getting his body moving. 'This was going to be an exciting day,' thought Petey. He reflected on his journey so far, today the first half of that journey would end. He could not control himself anymore; he circled back toward his friends and made a loud and wet splash right next to them. Startled, they both woke up.

"I guess you are awake," said Goggles.

"What's the big idea; can't you recognize a sleeping duck when you see one?" exclaimed Lucky.

Petey smiled to himself seeing Lucky half asleep.

"It's the big day!" exclaimed Petey, much too loud for the morning. "Today we arrive at the lake, right Goggles?" he inquired.

"You are right," replied Goggles, "though I could have enjoyed a little more shut eye first."

"Forget that," said Petey, "It's cold and I want to get moving." Petey's excitement was evident by his constant circling of his friends.

"It is cold," agreed Goggles, "okay, we can fly to Surprise now if you would like. But Petey, you better get used to the cold; it is April in New York. I have even seen snow this time of the year."

"Will I see more ice?"

"Yes, you will at the lake. Let's get going."

The three jumped into the cool air together and flew up the river. Before long, they circled away from the rising sun and left the river. Goggles seemed to know where he was going; below, the town of Coxsackie appeared. The town was just waking up as few cars were on the streets. The three headed over hills, around mountains and through valleys. Goggles looked back only once, the expressions on his friends' faces were sheer excitement.

Each pond or lake that Goggles took them over Petey thought was their lake. They seemed to cross many swamps and lakes, until finally Goggles started down to one. Flying over a swamp, then a grassy sidehill, Goggles honking increased and echoed off the hemlock stands along one side of the lake. The three made a splashdown into a swirling morning mist in the middle of Goggles' pond in Surprise, NY. Petey was speechless; he just listened as Goggles honked loudly, telling all around that he was back home. Petey and Lucky stayed off to the side, just watching Goggles as he swam proudly around in a display of joy.

Petey finally whispered to Lucky, "I never imagined this to be so pretty."

"It is nice," said Lucky.

"Goggles is in his own world right now. Why is he making all that noise?"

"He is calling for April, letting her know it is he, or at least the other geese if she is not here. It's a ritual."

"Oh, I figured."

Shortly Goggles was done with his display and he swam over to the pair.

"Do you like it my friends?"

"I can see why you come back every year, it is beautiful, quiet and peaceful." said Petey.

"It is not as fancy as some of the places we stay, but there is no better place to raise a family- much to eat and very safe."

"Where is April?" asked Petey.

"She will be here soon; sometimes her flock is a little later than ours."

"The trees are very bare. Why are there no leaves?" asked Petey.

"It is still early in the Spring; don't worry; there will be leaves soon; there will be many changes here in the next few months."

The group enjoyed their first meal together at their new home. Petey would have to get used to a salt free diet, though there was plenty of sunfish and bass to feed on. Many of the lake's birds would stop and watch Petey feed with his strange dives head first into the water.

That afternoon Petey went for a flight around by himself. He discovered the beaver swamps and hayfields that surrounded the lake. Upon his return, he saw another goose sitting next to Goggles on the lake. He splashed down and swam over.

"Petey, this is April, she is my life mate," said Goggles.

"So pleased to meet you April," said Petey.

"A pelican in New York," said April shaking her head, "and I thought Goggles was kidding me. Welcome Petey," said April.

"It is great to be here," smiled Petey.

Goggles spent the rest of the day explaining to April all the adventures the three had. Lucky had to tell of Petey's brush with the hawk in the rushes, to Petey's embarrassment. The four talked all day and into the night. By the time the four went to sleep, Petey felt that April was a part of the group, making it stronger still.

18
Petey's Summer Days

Goggles was right when he said there would be many changes throughout the summer. Summer in Surprise brought warm sunny days. The afternoons would occasionally bring a thunderstorm that echoed off the distant mountains. Nighttime belonged to the wide variety of sounds. The sound of peepers, bullfrogs, splashing of fish and soft rustling of night creatures would keep Petey awake for hours. While awake, Petey would look at the stars. The stars at Goggles' pond shone brighter than anywhere he had ever been.

Though Petey loved the sounds and peacefulness of his new home, it was the visitors he liked best. His favorite visitor was a little boy. The boy would come to sit on the side hills that surrounded the lake and fish. He would talk to Petey, so Petey would sit next to him. This helped Petey feel at home, like his time with the old man on the fishing pier. The boy never threw him a fish, but that was okay. Petey just wanted to watch him and be near. Some nights the boy would come with his family and start a fire on the shoreline. Petey would sit on the dock and listen to their conversations deep into the night.

Goggles and April had their goslings; there were six of them. Each one was cuter than the next. Goggles was a great father; he hissed at anything that would come near. One day the boy did come near; the boy would not do that again. With Goggles so busy, Petey and Lucky spent a lot of time  together. Lucky was always in the mood to fly around the swamps. Petey would fly with him, in and out of the trees; splashing down in some spooky looking areas. Lucky was changing a lot. One day Petey figured out why Lucky loved to fly into the swamp. On one flight, he saw a tiny duck sitting all alone on a quiet, well-sheltered opening in the swamp. She was looking toward Lucky as Petey flew by.

"Come on Lucky, lets go over there," shouted Petey.

"Naw, not today," said Lucky with an anxious look on his face.

"I am going without you then." And Petey banked toward the lone duck. Landing away from her, Petey paddled over.

"Hi," said Petey.

"Hello," replied the mallard.

"My name is Petey," continued Petey.

"My name is Crystal."

"It's nice to meet you," said Petey, "do you live here?"

"Why yes I do, I mean now I do; we moved here just recently from the Hudson River."

"I've been to the Hudson River," replied Petey.

Just then Lucky landed behind Petey.

"Oh," said Petey, "this is my friend Lucky. Lucky, this is Crystal, she just moved here."

"Pleased to meet you Crystal," said Lucky.

Petey looked at Lucky and smiled, "Oops" he faked, "I just heard Goggles, I had better go. Nice meeting you Crystal."

With that he jumped out of the water and was gone.

Petey did not see Lucky again for two weeks. When he did see him, it was by accident. While taking his evening flight, he spotted a duck that looked much like Lucky, sitting on a nest. Petey did not think he saw him, and continued on. With both of his friends love struck, Petey had time to himself. He would play with Goggles' children, harass frogs, take long flights and sit with the boy. The summer days moved on, every day a new adventure. Weeks and weeks passed.

April saw it first. She told Goggles and Goggles honked to Petey. Out of the woods they came: one by one, seven in all. Forming a straight line, Crystal second in line and Lucky sitting up straight at the front.

Lucky hardly looked like Lucky at all, a proud dad with his family behind him. Petey could barely keep from breaking out in laughter. Here was the same duck who was always playing practical jokes and getting into mischief, a dad. Lucky paddled over to Petey, and Goggle's family and stopped. With his own family in a perfectly straight line, they floated. He had a stoic, serious look on his face. Keeping his posture straight and proper, he closed his eyes and looked down his nose at his friends and started to talk… Before he could speak, he broke out into laughter, his posture fell apart and he returned to the same old Lucky. This brought a giggle from his ducklings behind him.

Lucky broke from the formation and shouted, "What are you laughing at, I'll get you!" as he chased them around in the lake. The ducklings were obviously used to this game and they scattered making funny faces at their dad. This brought laughter from everyone except Crystal. She sat shaking her head.

So that is how Lucky introduced his family to the world. Crystal would later say that he practiced the proper way for days and was all set. That is just Lucky, nothing proper about him.

Petey now had two families to play with; they kept him busy going from the lake to the swamp. One evening Lucky flew over to the lake to paddle with Petey.

"Hey Lucky, you have some time away from the family?"

"Yeah, Crystal is cleaning them all up, so I thought I would stop to see my best friend."

Petey looked up at him.

Lucky continued, "Petey, I owe everything to you. These past four months have been the greatest times of my life." Lucky paused. "I thought after the hurricane took my family I would never feel that way again. The reason I do is because of you- a silly pelican from Florida." Petey smiled.

Lucky continued, "I want to thank you, without you none of this is possible. You will always be my best friend."

Petey didn't know what to say; so, he said nothing. They fed together until the stars shone down on them.

"You better go Lucky, thanks for visiting. Enjoy your family while you can. Goggles said that we will be flying South in a short time from now."

"I know, they grow so fast and then it is back to us again. I'm looking forward to getting our traveling party together again."

"Me too, but not too soon."

"See ya."

"Goodnight," shouted Petey.

Petey thought of Lucky all night. Lucky really had changed. Everyone deserves a second chance- everyone.

19
Everything is Fragile

"When is the last time you saw Lucky?" asked Goggles.

"He stopped out to see me the other night, two days ago I think," Petey replied. "Why?"

"Do you know where in the swamp he is?"

"Yes, but why Goggles?" Petey repeated.

"I spoke to another family up the lake," Goggles offered, "they saw a fox this afternoon lurking near the swamp. They can be very dangerous, especially for ducklings. It is important that Lucky know that."

Their conversation came to an abrupt halt; the noise and commotion coming from the swamp startled the two friends. Crystal was flying with all her strength, crashing through the cattails to get to Goggles. In an instant, Petey's heart began to race, Crystal's expression did not require words. Petey jumped to the air and passed Crystal as she was yelling to Goggles. The three streaked toward the swamp with Petey in the lead. Petey landed hard into Lucky's pool. The crash landing sent water splashing everywhere. The frightened ducklings came to Petey when the water cleared; a quick count came up seven.

"Where is Lucky?" shouted Petey. "Lucky! Lucky!" shouted Petey as he franticly looked around.

He could not get into the air here; the brush around the swamp hole prevented it. He struggled up the muddy bank surrounding the water. When he got on the bank, he saw fresh footprints leading into the brush. In an emotional surge, he slammed with all his might into the thick brush on the bank. The brush was too thick to get through. Petey kept slamming as hard as he could, feathers flying off his wings as blood began to trickle down his beak. Finally the brush broke open and Petey was on the forest floor. He looked up in time to see the startled fox jump over the ledges and out of sight. A feather floated gently to the ground. Petey lay on the forest floor, muddy, disheveled and bleeding. The sounds of Crystal crying, and Goggles trying to soothe her were mixed with Petey's heavy breathing and heartbeat. Petey could not believe what had just happened, Lucky was gone.

20
The Heavy Heart of Friendship

Many say that time heals all wounds; Petey doubted it. In fact, he hated time. He knew time would not replace Lucky. So what good was it. Petey did not understand why this had to happen. Everything was going great for his friend, why? This was a question that no matter how much he traveled he would never be able to answer. He even tried flight. Flight always answered questions. Not this one. One time Petey wished he never took this stupid adventure. Who did he think he was anyway? The gang back in Florida did not have to feel this way. The whole thing made him mad. Why Lucky?

As if knowing Petey's feelings, the weather on the lake was changing. The evenings were cooler and the winds began to blow. Mother nature changed the colors on the trees to try to cheer him up. The stars shone much brighter at night and the boy came to visit more often. Time and the lake did help him to see things better. He learned to focus on the time he had with Lucky, not the time he won't have. It didn't take the pain away, but it did make things a little better. Crystal did a great job raising the ducklings; they brought him some comfort.

Goggles' family grew up; April was going to take them to her flock for the winter. Goggles liked his independence; April always knew that. One day April said her goodbyes and they were gone.

"When are we going to leave?" asked Petey.

"When you are ready old friend; it will get colder but we still have time."

"Won't the flock be getting together?"

"Yes, shortly; we have time though," replied Goggles.

"You have learned a lot in Surprise, huh Petey?"

"Yes I have," sighed Petey.

"Do you wish you were still a Salty?" inquired Goggles.

"Sometimes I do, but most of the time I am thankful," replied Petey.

"You are growing up Petey. Life is not ever going to be the same! Growing up is about experiences, both good and bad. I am sorry for your friend, and I am sorry for how you feel. But this experience, as well as the traveling, is what life is all about. I admire and look up to you, Petey. You are much more than most Pelicans."

Goggles went silent for a time.

He continued, "Your wonder is what makes you special. With wonder comes these experiences, but also with wonder comes a rich, fulfilling life."

"Thank you Goggles, I am thankful for the experiences. I am also thankful to have a friend like you." The two slapped wings and fed by the dying light of the evening.

On an absolutely beautiful fall morning, the two said goodbye to the lake in Surprise. They flew three laps around the lake and were off to the Hudson River to meet the rest of the V. Petey glanced over his shoulder, his eyes lingering on the swamp where Lucky spent his days. A tear came to his eyes.

21
Big Changes

Most of the flock had already assembled. Goggles brought them down to the middle of the flock floating in a small inlet along the river. The familiar sounds of their former traveling partners brought comfort to Petey. The flock immediately noticed there was no Lucky. Goggles explained everything, while Petey sat silent. The flock was very sympathetic and said many kind words about Lucky. Petey felt good to talk about his old friend and share some funny stories. The flock ate heartedly for a few days while waiting for the rest of the leaders. Goggles did see his uncle fly in; he knew it would not be long now. Petey was getting sick of all the fresh water fish; he longed for some Salty catches and was anxious to get moving.

To everyone's surprise, on Goggle's and Petey's second day back with the flock, Goggles' uncle called a meeting scheduled to follow the evening feeding. The flock assembled to hear from the leader. Nobody was prepared for what he was going to say.

"Good evening flock, you might have noticed that the other leaders are not present this evening. I regret to inform you that we will be making some changes. I have received notice this afternoon that the remaining leaders will not be accompanying us back to Florida. The journey is too much for them to lead and they will be joining another flock for the return. Therefore, it is my duty to assign new leaders for the flight back. With much discussion with the elders of the flock and some thought, I am prepared to offer two new leaders to join me up front."

The flock grew very quiet. All were alert and excited.

"Of course, they would need to agree to this difficult task, but I am prepared to ask for your approval and their acceptance."

A pause for effect, then he continued.

"The flock of the Hudson Valley of Upstate New York requests the services of Goggles and Petey to be our new leaders!"

Goggle's ears began to ring; his head began to swim; he felt he would black out. Petey slapped his back with a hearty thump, which pulled him out of his downward spiral.

"Can you believe it?!" shouted Petey over the honking of approval from the flock.

As Goggles started to come around a broad smile crossed his face.

The honking and splashing continued as Goggles' uncle shouted over the noise, "Will you two come forward?"

Goggles and Petey paddled to the front and the noise quieted.

"Well boys, will you accept?"

Silence... still more silence, finally Goggles' uncle spoke again.

"You may speak to a leader," he offered.

Goggles spoke, "I am," he corrected himself, "we are honored you put your trust in us. We would gladly lead this flock, but we would like to make some changes."

This caught Goggles' uncle off guard.

"That is highly irregular, changes are not our way," he said.

"With all the respect of a leader sir, I do not think the old leaders would have had a pelican lead the flock either," Goggles stated.

"Very well," he said with a smile, "what change would you have?"

"That any flock member talk to us leaders any time they would like without asking permission. We are one as a flock, and all suggestions are welcome. We may lead, but we are no more important than any other member of our flock."

The flock broke out in cheers, so loud that Goggles' uncle would not even attempt to talk over them. He nodded his head yes, and the two friends smiled at each other.

22
Flight Home

Petey and Goggles, with Goggles' uncle, made the decision to fly out the next day. A strong snow squall started up on the river and blanketed the shoreline with a dusting of white crystals. Before leaving, Petey became the first Pelican to catch snowflakes on his tongue. With the wind at their backs, the flock seemed to cover a lot of ground. Goggles said the fall winds were helping them to fly very fast, much faster than the spring winds. Petey enjoyed all the responsibilities and planning that comes with being a leader. What he did not like was how hard it was to fly in the front. They would take turns so nobody would have to work too hard.

Petey also began to enjoy night flights. With the harvest moon so full and the strong breezes at night, the flock chose to fly mostly at night. This was a beautiful experience, the twinkling lights below and the full white moon above made time and miles go by so quickly.

Goggles would smile to himself when he imagined all the geese sitting below, watching up as his flock crossed the moon. In front there was the unmistakable shape of a pelican leading the way. It seemed so long ago that

Petey splashed in his pond in Florida and he scolded him. He felt bad about how he behaved back then, calling him, of all birds, a Salty. A Salty he was not; he was a true friend and lifelong traveling companion.

Every day the weather grew warmer. Goggles' uncle was taking less time in the lead so Goggles and Petey had to work harder. They did not mind, but Petey was sure tired at the end of the day.

On their travels, they were sure to stop and tell Lucky's friends of the tragic news. Rasty and Gorry were sad but tried to share uplifting stories to hide the pain. Sergeant Stuffy had a proper military funeral, complete with a 21-gun salute and memorial set up on his island.

There were little problems on the return. The leaders did a fine job directing the flock, and slowly they approached Longboat Key.

23
Back Home

Horace sat idly, the warm sun warming his head and back. The roads and water were getting busier, 'must be getting colder up north,' he thought. The distant sound of gulls and water slapping against the pier was soothing.

Suddenly a brown streak appeared. It was Bungles, flying much too fast to land on the pier pylon next to him. He overshot his landing and tripped, landing face first onto the pier, and then sliding forward where he slipped into the water below the pylon with a splash. He righted himself and began to hurriedly speak; nothing but water came out. Shaking his head, he cleared his mouth and managed to blurt out,

"Look to the north!"

Horace whipped around and saw what Bungles was excited about. There, flying across the bay, was a V of geese, each goose honking just as loud as they could, making more racket than Horace had ever heard a flock make. As the V approached, Horace could not believe his eyes, there leading the flock was his good buddy, Petey.

"Welcome home," Horace whispered to himself, "I sure missed you."

The End.

About the Author

Douglas Lampman resides in Surprise, NY with his wife, children and his hunting dog. He works for a local construction company in the summer and teaches high school physical education during the school year. He also coaches boys basketball and is a department leader at his school. His hobbies include coaching, hunting, fishing, sports, carpentry, snowmobiling, listening to music, playing guitar, farming, cooking and spending time with family and friends. With a real passion for travel and new experiences, he hopes to spend his days of retirement seeing the world with his lovely wife Stephanie.

About the Illustrators

E dmund Brennan was born in 1935 in Manhattan, New York City. Ned is married to Margaret and raised seven children. Ned served five years in the US Military and seventeen years in the New York Police Department. Ned enjoys drawing, gardening, spending time with his sixteen grandchildren and traveling. Ned and his beautiful wife enjoy getting out of the city to spend time in Surprise, NY and traveling.

W endy Doney resides in the town of Catskill where she and her husband, Brian, have raised three awesome children. Wendy is employed by the Catskill Central School District where she teaches high school and college art. She is also an active member of the Greene County Council on the Arts where she helps to promote the importance of art.

Wendy enjoys drawing and painting, hiking, and participating in the community; teaching workshops as well as exhibiting her artwork in gallery shows and local establishments.

CPSIA information can be obtained
at www.ICGtesting.com
Printed in the USA
LVHW041057270519
619152LV00003B/448/P